Doo-Dad

(A Feral Cat Who Took a Chance on Love)

Martha Hostnick

Copyright © 2017 Martha Hostnick
All rights reserved
First Edition

PAGE PUBLISHING, INC.
New York, NY

First originally published by Page Publishing, Inc. 2017

ISBN 978-1-63568-815-3 (Paperback)
ISBN 978-1-63568-816-0 (Digital)

Printed in the United States of America

Dedication

"This book is dedicated to Dr Alexander V. Freyman, Sanford Veterinary Hospital, Sanford, FL, without whose help DooDad would not be alive today."

This story is about Doo-Dad and his amazing two-year journey from a feral cat to a loving member of our family.

I first saw Doo-Dad in June of 2013. He was hiding in the backyard between our fence and that of the adjoining property. He was very skinny with bones showing and had an odd-shaped face. I realized he had folded-down ears and must be a Scottish Fold cat. I couldn't imagine how a cat like this had ended up outside to fend for himself. I was determined to help this kitty.

I walked toward the fence with a bowl of kitty food, but he ran down the alley toward a vacant home and hid in the bushes and then under the house. I left the bowl of food and water near the back steps of the vacant house and walked back across the alley to my house. Doo-Dad would not come out until he could no longer see me. I continued to feed Doo-Dad twice daily, moving closer to the vacant house, sitting on a low stool, talking to him each day for an hour morning and night so he would get used to me and the sound of my voice. This continued for a month or more. I was able to get within eight feet of Doo-Dad, but it was evident that he was very feral as he growled and hissed at me every time I put down his food and sometimes attacked me. I started wearing leather knee boots in the middle of summer and wearing a towel across my lap for protection.

Pretty soon it was time to leave for North Carolina to visit my sister. I tried catching Doo-Dad before I left, but I was unsuccessful. I worried about leaving Doo-Dad, but my husband, Michael, would be there to feed him while I was gone. Ultimately, Michael was successful in getting Doo-Dad across the alley and into our backyard to be fed. He also at this time was the one that named him Doo-Dad. Michael soon had to leave for North Carolina. He left food feeders and water feeders and hoped that he would be able to catch food on his own or that other neighbors would feed him until we got back.

We were away from home for a few months, and when we came back, we didn't see Doo-Dad right away. Michael continued to whistle for him morning and evening, and finally on the second day, Doo-Dad slowly walked into our backyard. He appeared to have a left hind quarter injury as he was holding his hind leg up as he limped along.

I started feeding him three times a day, talking to him again every morning and evening to get him used to my voice again. We decided to try to catch Doo-Dad to get him some medical help. We tried several times, but no luck. Doo-Dad was street-smart and was able to get the food out of the cage by tipping it over and not getting caught. We caught and released another cat and a small possum, but no Doo-Dad. Although Doo-Dad was eating three meals a day, he still was not gaining weight.

We continued with this same pattern for the next year and a half, leaving periodically to go to North Carolina and returning, each time not knowing if Doo-Dad would make it until we returned. Each time we returned, I would feed Doo-Dad three times a day and sit and talk to him for an hour at each feeding to let him know that he was loved and how brave he was to have survived each day in spite of his injuries. He also had a mangled left ear that was healed and misshaped from prior injuries.

In March of 2015, when we returned home, we did not see Doo-Dad for several days. We were heartbroken and thought he must have died. We whistled and called for two or three days. Finally on the fourth day, Doo-Dad appeared in our backyard. After that he would show up like clockwork for morning and evening feedings, but he was still very feral. We could not touch him or move suddenly while feeding him or he would attack us, biting and/or scratching. I was very determined to try to catch this kitty if possible and get him some much needed help.

We had to return to North Carolina for a few weeks, but while we were there, I worried about this little boy who continued to survive no matter what was thrown at him. He deserved love, a warm bed, and food every day, not just when we were there. We came home in a few weeks, but in the meantime, while we were gone, Doo-Dad was in a fight with a possum that was residing under the vacant house across the alley. His head was scalped from under one ear across the forehead to the other ear with fur and skin hanging and pus running down the side of his head. He must have been in so much pain. In a few days, the skin and fur fell off, leaving an open wound two inches by four inches.

I was desperate to get help from a veterinarian. I called several veterinary offices, but no one would prescribe medicine without first seeing the cat. I went online to see if I could give a cat amoxicillin and what dosage per pound. I calculated Doo-Dad's approximate weight and, based on the information I had found, took an amoxicillin capsule and divided it into fourths and gave a small dosage of the powder in his food at each meal to try to jump-start the healing process on his head wound until I could find a vet that would help me.

A friend of mine recommended her vet. I took a picture of Doo-Dad's injuries and went to the vet's office. I waited for some time until he could see me. I showed him a picture of Doo-Dad's wounds and asked him to please help me catch this cat. He gave me a pill to put in Doo-Dad's food that would make him drowsy enough that we could pick him up and bring him to the doctor. The next day I ground up one tablet and put it in Doo-Dad's food and watched him eat. An hour later, Doo-Dad was still wide awake. Three hours later, Doo-Dad was still wide awake.

The next day I went back to the doctor's office to get two pills. I ground up the pills and put them in Doo-Dad's food again and waited. A couple of hours later, Doo-Dad looked asleep. When we approached him, up he bounced and jumped the fence. When he came back later, I followed him around the neighborhood hoping he would lie down and go to sleep. He finally decided to lie down but went under a neighbor's house where I was unable to get to him. I called the vet's office and told him what was going on. We decided that I would need to get Doo-Dad to come onto our back porch to eat. That way he would fall asleep on the porch and I would be able to catch him.

For the next two weeks I worked with Doo-Dad each day, getting him to come closer to the inside of the enclosed back porch. At first he would only eat on the steps. Finally I got him to come partway into the back porch but not enough to be able to close the door. I continued each day until the day came that I was able to get him into the middle of the back porch. I fed Doo-Dad his food with the ground-up pill in it, and while Doo-dad was eating, closed the back door, and then waited in the house for forty-five minutes until Doo-Dad was asleep. An hour later, with help from a friend, I was successful in getting Doo-Dad into a carrier, and I was on the way to the veterinarian's office.

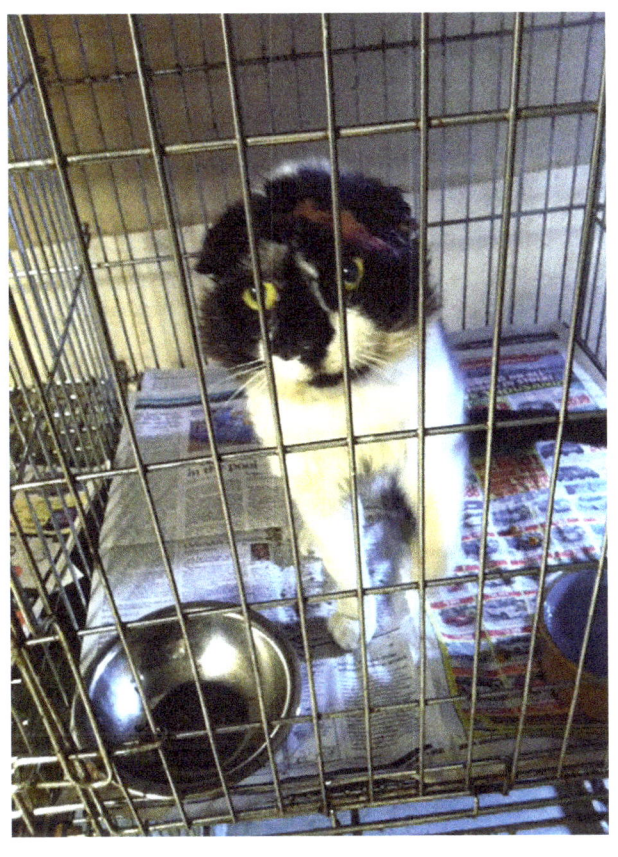

After discussions with the vet, we agreed that we would first give Doo-Dad a much needed bath, neuter him, check for a chip, and draw blood to make sure he wasn't positive for feline leukemia and check for heartworms. A couple of hours later I called to see how Doo-dad was doing. He was so badly infested with fleas that he had needed two baths, had a tapeworm in his intestines and his ears were infested with ear mites. Otherwise, he was doing well from the surgery. A day after surgery, I took some cat food to the vet's office, since I knew how much Doo-Dad loved his Fancy Feast Classic kitty food. When Doo-Dad heard my voice, he got up in his cage and meowed for me. I went to him and tried to feed him, but again he attacked and scratched. He wanted love so much but didn't know how to go about getting it. Every day until Doo-Dad came home, I visited him at the vet's office so he would know I had not abandoned him. After seven days I took Doo-Dad home and kept him inside until he was well enough to go back outside.

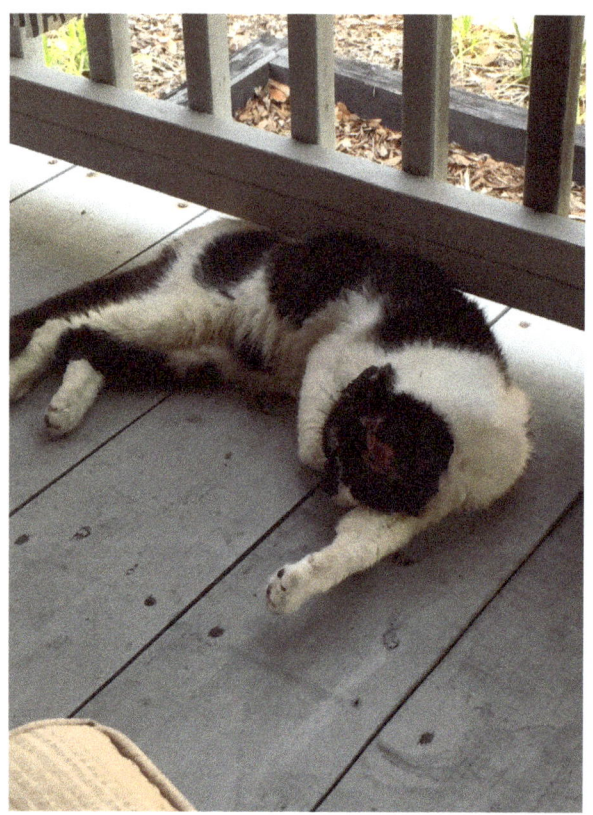 

In the meantime, I had made a place for him to sleep on our covered front porch instead of under the house. I had a nice bed enclosed on three sides so he would feel safe, food and water bowls, a love seat to sit on with his own quilt to lie on and a fan to keep him cool since it was the middle of summer and so hot on the porch. After four or five days of being inside, I put Doo-Dad on the front porch with his food bowl and sat with him for an hour and talked to him telling him what a brave boy he was. That evening, I repeated the same thing, sitting with him for an hour talking to him. The next morning I opened the front door to feed him and he was at the back door again. I walked around to the back, enticing him with food to come to the front of the house so he would get used to me coming out the front door to feed him. Doo-Dad was feeling better, but he still attacked me regularly every time I tried to give him his food bowl or take the dirty bowl away.

In spite of continued attacks, I was still determined that I would win this cat over with love and patience. After many bloody attacks, I decided to go to the local pet store and looked at various pheromone products and found one called Stop That, a cat pheromone that stops unwanted behavior. I bought a can and brought it home ready to try at the next feeding. I walked out with the food bowl and bent over to put the bowl down and at the same time spraying Stop That. Doo-Dad immediately stopped his aggressive attack and backed up and looked at me. I was able to put the food bowl down and pick up the dirty bowls. I was so elated and encouraged that this just might work. Every morning and night when I fed Doo-Dad and sat down with him, I sprayed the pheromone with success.

Doo-Dad was on prescribed antibiotics and was given them each day in his food. As the days continued, Doo-Dad's wound was slowly closing up. Part of his fur had slowly grown back, but not very thick. Part of the scar would never grow hair back. Where the ear mites had been, there were very few wisps of hair. About a couple of weeks later, each time after he finished eating, he would come over to me in front of my chair and just sit at my feet looking me in the eyes. I kept talking to him, telling him what a good boy he was and how brave he had been and told him he just had to try to be a little braver and try to trust me a little further. That he would never have to worry about his next meal, a place to sleep, or confrontations with other cats. We continued this way for a few more days with Doo-Dad each day sitting at my feet, lying on his quilt, or sitting looking me in the eyes while I talked with him. Sometimes he would lie down at my feet and go to sleep, but never ventured any closer.

One evening, Doo-Dad came over to me after eating and rubbed on my boots back and forth as he paced. I told him, "Oh, you trust me a little to rub on my boots for affection, but not enough for me to touch you." I told him that was OK, that I was not rushing him. That we had already gone through the worst with his injuries and he was on his way to becoming healthy and putting on weight. He sat down and looked at me with piercing eyes, and I told him, "I think I know what you are thinking, but are you ready to jump into my lap?" He didn't jump into my lap that night, but each day he would look into my eyes longer and longer and rub on my boots. We continued in this manner of eating, talking, and him rubbing on my boots. I couldn't touch him yet. If I moved too quickly, he would scratch or bite my boots or shirtsleeve, sometimes puncturing my arm.

The next day after he was finished eating and he was sitting at my feet, I decided to read my Kindle and looked away for a minute. In that instant, Doo-Dad took a flying leap over the arm of the chair and was in my lap. I held my breath, not knowing whether he would attack me or bite me. I talked very softly to Doo-Dad, telling him I was so proud of him for taking a leap of faith and telling him that I was going to pet him. I took one finger and touched his head lightly, not making any unusual moves. He allowed my touch, and within a few minutes, I heard this faint noise, a small, quiet purr. I asked Doo-Dad, "Is that a purr I hear?" We had reached a milestone in our relationship. By this time, I was crying and called my friend and husband and said, "Guess who's sitting in my lap."

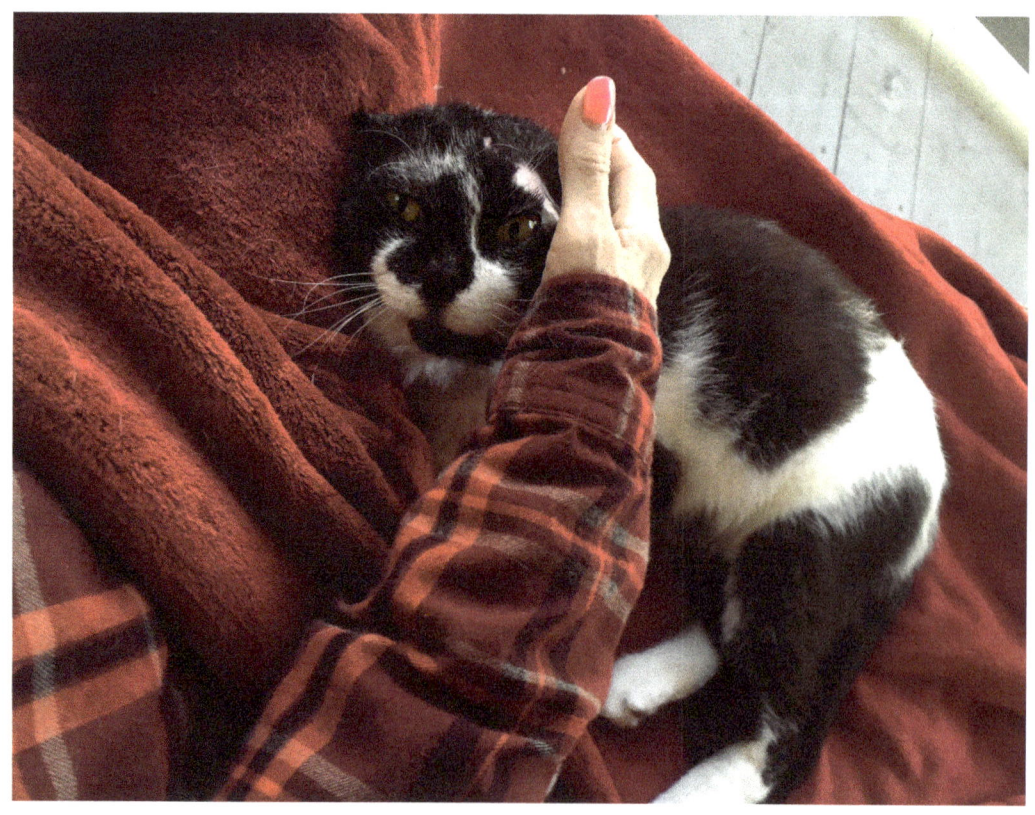

I continued the daily feedings and conversations with Doo-Dad eating and then jumping on the love seat snuggling up to my lap or crawling into my lap with my petting him. He still would occasionally scratch or bite my shirt or me, especially when I got up to leave him to go inside for the evening. He wanted affection now more than food. I had to sit close to him while he ate and then tap my lap for him to hop up. At this point he was still an outside cat.

In a couple of months, I had to return North Carolina for a few weeks. I made arrangements with a friend that Doo-Dad knew for her to come over to the house every other day to feed him, filling up his two automatic feeders and water bowls. She would also sit with Doo-Dad for an hour talking to him and petting him. She called me every other day to report on Doo-Dad and said Doo-Dad was so lonely and that he needed to be made part of our household and become an inside cat. I came home from North Carolina in the fall of 2015, and after discussions with my veterinarian, we decided to have Doo-Dad declawed since my other rescue cat, Sophie, was declawed when I got her.

We scheduled the surgery and very shortly brought Doo-Dad home to live with us in the house. Doo-Dad still was not totally well. The tapeworm had come back, and we put him on another round of medicines. He continued to eat constantly but still did not gain weight. We gave him another medicine to clean out any parasites left in his system and did blood work to rule out anything else. The blood work came back normal, and after the second round of parasite medicine, Doo-Dad was on the road to recovery.

Since his surgery and becoming an inside kitty, Doo-Dad has become a most loving kitty wanting nothing else but to sit in your lap, snuggle up next to my chin, or lie next to you while you pet him. His aggression has totally subsided, and he and Sophie have learned to walk politely around each other. Occasionally I hear galloping through the house at three in the morning as they play. Doo-Dad is submissive to Sophie, lying down at her feet after they touch noses and sniff each other. Doo-Dad has learned to play for the first time with his toys, and I can hear him in the middle of the night batting his toys around. What a joy it is to see Doo-Dad play. When he sits in my lap or crawls up on my chest and lays his head on my shoulder looking in my eyes and purring his little heart out, my heart sings, all because Doo-Dad, a feral cat, took chance on love.

Update: 2016

Doo-Dad gets more loving as time goes on. He loves playing with toys and sleeps with us in our bed part of the night and spends the rest in the kitty side porch with Sophie. They have become kissing buddies and often lie close to each other. He never meows unless he is going to the vet. Instead he comes up to you quietly purring his heart out and lightly taps you on the arm or chest to let you know he is hungry or would like some snack. He still eats four meals a day but never more than a full can a day. He likes his little midnight snack to tide him through the night.

He continues to amaze me as to his transformation from a mean feral cat to the most loving cat I have ever owned. Some people have said that he's not very pretty, and some have called him ugly, but when I look at the little face turned up to me with those bright eyes, purring softly, all I see is this beautiful little boy that was determined to survive despite all his injuries and had the courage to try on a daily basis to trust me more and more until he finally took a chance on me and accepted love.

Doo-Dad is a survivor, and as it turns out, he's not young. He's a senior, about ten years old. Every day Doo-Dad lets me know how much he loves me and appreciates his home. He purrs constantly before you ever pick him up. He follows me everywhere and climbs up in bed every night and lays his little head on my shoulder purring. Doo-Dad is my precious miracle boy.

I am so happy that Doo-Dad is part of my life. We have had quite a journey together, one that I will never forget. I have become a better person while traveling on this road with Doo-Dad.

About the Author

The author was born in Erie, Pennsylvania, and went to school there until the fourth grade when her family moved to a farm in another part of the state. She enjoyed living on a farm because she loved animals and wanted to help any animal that was injured. They had dogs, geese, chickens, pigs, and lots of rabbits. They moved to Florida when she was eleven years old. She continued to nurture animals whenever possible and had a dog, Maggie, who was a family pet.

When she found and rescued Doo-Dad, her life was changed by the two-year journey that he allowed her to take with him and was compelled to tell his heartwarming story. He has taught her what real courage is and how patience and love can overcome any obstacle.

She is currently living in the Central Florida area with her husband Michael and their two cats. One of course is Doo-Dad, and the other is Sophie, a Maine Coone rescue cat. The two of them sleep together, whisker to whisker, or in the same kitty room together. She has been fortunate to be blessed with two loving cats, both of whom are very quiet and do not meow. Sophie talks to you with her eyes and makes you follow her to tell you what she wants. Doo-Dad comes up to you and purrs loudly in your ear and gently taps you on the arm or shoulder to let you know that he needs something, usually food or snack, or just more love. It is such a joy to listen to Doo-Dad playing with toys, even though it is the middle of the night.

What a rewarding experience rescuing any animal can be. Her heart is always open to the next rescue kitty that may come her way.

Lightning Source UK Ltd.
Milton Keynes UK
UKHW050924161220
375218UK00003B/87